READ·BY·YOURSELF

BOOKS

Mary E. Kullberg

illustrated by

MARIA A. BOES

HOUGHTON MIFFLIN COMPANY • Boston

BILL'S GREAT TRICK

New York · Atlanta · Geneva, Ill. · Dallas · Palo Alto

This is Kay-o the Great, dressed in yellow and blue.

Kay-o has many good tricks he can do.

The children all like to come here, for they know
That Kay-o the Great has a very good show.
"Watch now," the children once heard Kay-o say,
"For this is the very best trick of the day —
I will now pull a rabbit named Bill from this hat!"
How the children all laughed

when great Kay-o did that!

But Bill was not laughing — he looked very sad.

Being pulled from a hat every day made him mad.

"I know what I'll do," said Bill, "I'll go away.

Then I'll do nothing but eat, sleep, and play."

Just outside town was a field that was green,

The best place to live that Bill ever had seen.

There Bill did as he wanted —

he jumped, hopped, and ran.

And he lay in the sun, till he had a good tan.

For a while Bill had fun in his field,

> green and sunny.

But one day he said to himself, "This is funny.

I came here so I would have nothing to do,

But now I find out I am tired of this, too!"

Bill hopped on the fence to think what he could do —

Something great, something fun,

> something ever so new!

14

"I have it!" he shouted. "I know what I'll do.
It's great and it's fun and it's ever so new.
I'll learn how to pull a man out of a hat.
I'm sure that no rabbit has ever done that!"

The next morning Bill woke up early at six.

He hopped into town, and he looked all around

Till he found the right place to learn how

to do tricks.

"Now I'll find books on tricks," Bill said to himself.

And there by the door he saw just the right shelf.

He stayed a long time reading big books and small.

Red, green, and blue books, and Bill read them all.

18

In the very last book, on page one twenty-two

He found how to do what he wanted to do.

"To pull a man out of a hat," the book said,

"You must say these five words as you stand

on your head,

ZOO   ZOO   ZEE   ZEE   ZAIR!"

Bill kept saying the words as he ran out the door.

So he wouldn't forget them, he said them some more.

Outside, on the sidewalk, Bill started to call,

"Come and see, come and see the best show of all!"

The people came running when they heard Bill shout.

They wanted to see what the shout was about.

Bill kept calling and calling, "Come over and see —

No one can do this great trick but me!"

"What's all this noise?" asked two men

dressed in blue.

"Who dares to make all of this hul-la-ba-loo?"

"I guess I did make too much noise," said poor Bill.

"But this is so good that I cannot keep still.

Just stay for my show, it's a great show," said Bill.

"I'll pull a man out of your hat! Yes, I will!"

"Now that is a good joke! HO! HO!"

laughed one man.

"Well, let's see you pull out a man, if you can."

But the other man said, "Don't forget, if you fail,

For making so much noise, we'll put you in jail."

Was Bill scared? Yes, he was!

And he looked very pale

For he knew he would never be happy in jail.

But he tried it — he held the man's hat in the air

And he called out these words,

"ZOO ZOO ZEE ZEE ZAIR!"

27

It was not a man that Bill pulled from that hat,
But a bear playing golf with a baseball and bat!

Two frogs playing leapfrog —

Three dogs doing tricks —

Four monkeys, all hopping on red pogo-sticks —

Five flying squirrels —

Six raccoons on balloons —

Seven cats eating catnip with big wooden spoons —

Eight ducks with umbrellas, in case it might rain,

Nine little brown mice in a tiny toy train.

"What a spot I am in now!" poor Bill Rabbit cried,

"If I don't pull a man out, they WILL think I lied.

What could have gone wrong with my

clever new plan?

I'll just change the words."

Did he pull out a man?

No! Out jumped ten green-as-grass rabbits instead,

And each of the green rabbits stood on Bill's head.

"On my head!" shouted Bill.

"That was what that book said.

When I say the right words, I must stand on my head."

So he stood on his head with his feet in the air,

And once more he shouted,

"ZOO ZOO ZEE ZEE ZAIR!"

"Hooray! Hip, Hooray!" all the shouting began,

For this time Bill did it, he pulled out a man!

The man dressed in blue cried, "Did you all see that?

That rabbit DID pull a man out of my hat!"

Bill should have been happy, he should have been glad.

But was he? He was not.

Said Bill, "This looks bad —

Is it Kay-o the Great that I pulled from the hat?"

It WAS Kay-o the Great, and he said with a roar,

"You won't pull ME out of a hat any more."

Bill said, "You pulled ME from a hat every day,

And I did not like it. So I ran away."

Then Kay-o said, "Bill, please come back to the show.

Pulling you from a hat is the best trick I know.

If you do come back now, I will promise you that

You and I will take turns being pulled from the hat."

Bill said, "I will do it!" Then up came two men.
They shouted, "Hooray!" They picked Bill up and then
They held him up high, and did not put Bill down
Till they had paraded all over the town.

Behind came the animals pulled from the hat —

The bear playing golf with the baseball and bat —

The frogs playing leapfrog —

The dogs doing tricks —

The monkeys, all hopping on red pogo-sticks.

The high-flying squirrels, and then the raccoons,

And the cats eating catnip with big wooden spoons.

Then the ducks with umbrellas — it never did rain,
And the brown mice came pushing

their little toy train.

61

Ten busy green rabbits ran here and ran there.

They were taking men's hats and were calling,

"ZOO ZAIR!"

Why do you think the green rabbits did that?

Were they trying to pull a man out of a hat?

And in the parade, keeping each one in place,

Was Kay-o the Great with a smile on his face.

"Is it true?" said one man. "Is it true

what they say?

That Bill pulled a man out of a hat here today?"

"It is true!" another man said. "Just ask me,

I was here for the show. I'm from K Z X O

And I'm going to see that Bill gets on T.V.!"

63

Bill Rabbit is happy because he DID do

Something great, something fun,

                something ever so new!

Did you like Bill's show?

Well, now you know that a rabbit can

Pull a man out of a hat!